MOMMY

DADDY

BABY

Greg Kearney

Library and Archives Canada Cataloguing in Publication Data

Kearney, Greg
    Mommy, daddy, baby / Greg Kearney.

Short stories.
ISBN 1-894692-09-8

    I. Title.

PS8621.E37M65 2004   C813'.6   C2004-904331-5

Editor: Hal Niedzviecki
Copy editor: Ann Decter
Cover illustration: Shary Boyle
Cover design: Leif Harmsen
Inside design: Heather Guylar
Author photograph: David Hawe

McGilligan Books gratefully acknowledges the support of the
Canada Council for the Arts, the Ontario Arts Council and the
Ontario Book Publishers Tax Credit for our publishing program.

Canada Council   Conseil des Arts
for the Arts   du Canada

ONTARIO ARTS COUNCIL
CONSEIL DES ARTS DE L'ONTARIO

For the Danielson women, Arlene and Doreen.

STORIES

The Cat Gift 7

Anne Boleyn 11

Home Alarm 15

Rape and Kill 21

In Plum 27

Anchored in Hope 31

Blue Glass 37

Twice 43

Babysit 47

Flora 51

The Spell 55

Frank and Trudy 59

I Turn Devil 65

Shattered Vagina 69

Listen to This 75

Burning Lisbon 79

The Bookstore 83

Weights Are the Dirtiest Things 87

EVIL 93

Nook 97

My Tree-Tree 101

Uncommon Pink Softness 105

Three Beards 109

Luuuuuuve 113

Shalimar 117

Oh! 121

Mrs. Park 127

Love is the Wrong Kind of Nuance 133

Grab and Grab 139

THE CAT GIFT

The stooped man buys a cat at the pet store. The lady takes it out of its cage and smiles and tries to bring it close to the man's face.

Get the hell away from me! the man says. Just put it in a fucking box.

The man drops the box and slams the front door. His wife wakes with a start on the couch.

Oh! Don't do that, she says.

Don't do what? Come home?

She looks at him with wide eyes. He looks at her, his eyes slits.

What's in the box?

What's in the box? I'll show you what's in the box.

The stooped man stoops down to flip open the flaps on the box. The cat peeks out, stone still.

Oh, no, the wife says. Oh no, no, no. You didn't!

Oh, yes, yes, yes! the man says. I did!

She gets up, runs through the house.

Get it away from me!

The man picks up the cat by its front haunches. Chases after his wife.

Come and pet the pretty cat, he says, taking the stairs two at a time. On the top step is his wife's pink slipper. She runs into the bedroom. Throws herself on the bed.

You know I hate cats! They're awful! They terrify me! Please!

The man holds the cat over her. Its back paws kick and jut.

Pet it! the man screams. He rubs the cat's back against her face.

I'm going crazy! I'm dying! the wife says, but she doesn't move away. I'm going to shit from horror! Oh help me, Jesus!

Cat in the house, the man says. Nice surprise, eh?

Please Raymond! the wife says. She brings her hands together, palm to palm, like a little girl praying. My life! My love! *Please!*

The cat goes limp. The stooped man tries to straighten himself.

Why do I try? he says. Turns and walks out of the bedroom, down the stairs and out the front door. On the stoop he drops the cat, pushes it with his foot. It runs across the street. Up the neighbour's mailbox. Across the lawn. Behind a shed and into the bush.

I don't know what I'm doing, the man says. What am I doing?

He goes back inside. In the kitchen, his wife is holding a pack of bacon.

Why not bacon? she says. I always forget about bacon. I eat, and then I think, what about bacon? Bacon?

The man nods. Yes, bacon.

ANNE BOLEYN

The book is bigger than her lap. An old lady, following sentences with her finger.

Her daughter comes home. Box of adult diapers under one arm. Big macramé purse in the other.

Did you know, the old lady says, that Anne Boleyn had three breasts? And eleven fingers?

Did anyone call?

When?

Today. When I was out.

I don't know.

Did the phone ring?

It might have. I was reading. It's so interesting.

The daughter drops her purse. Bottles clink.

It's time for your bath.

But I just had one this morning.

And you stink again. I could smell you from the car.

You could not. Don't say that.

It's time for your bath.

The daughter digs one hand under the legs and one under a damp armpit. Rocks and lifts. The old lady wraps an arm around the daughter's shoulders. The other dangles, grazes the fern, the bureau.

She sets her in the bathtub and turns on the water. Hot tap.

Too hot! I'm scalded!

Cold tap.

The daughter goes into the kitchen. Looks at all her high heels, lined up on the boot mat. Picks them up, shoe by shoe. Throws them in the front closet. Sees her machine. Blinking. Hits play.

It's Wendy O'Brien from homecare. It's now after two. I was told you'd be home for me. Umm. I'll call at four.

Hi. It's Brenda. Bunch of us are off to karaoke tonight. The usual. I'm sure you're busy up the ass. Anyhoo. Love to you and your mum. We'll all do a shot in your honour. Bye. Oh yeah, they have to take the rest of my teeth out. Can you believe it? Oh well. Doesn't Jeanne Moreau have dentures? 'kay. Take care.

It's Wendy O'Brien again. It is now after four. This is hugely inconvenient. I have sixteen other patients to see today. I'll try you again in an hour. Please be home. And please, don't let this happen again.

It's almost at the rim, calls the old lady.

The daughter stomps back into the bathroom. Turns off the taps. Grabs for shampoo. Bar soap. Liquid soap.

You couldn't turn off the tap?

The daughter is sweating.

I'm in homecare. I need to be taken care of.

The daughter kneels, dips a washcloth in the water. Scrubs the back and bony shoulders. Scrubs the empty breasts, taking each one in her hand.

Anne Boleyn's head was chopped off and everyone thought she was not too nice, the old lady says. But do you know who her daughter was? Heh? Huh? Heh?

Who? The daughter grabs an arm.

Queen Elizabeth. The first one. And she was the queen for a long time. But she was a virgin. They called her The Virgin Queen.

I know that. Quit moving. You're stirring up the stink.

I don't stink.

Fine. You don't stink. But you stink.

After the bath the daughter carries the old lady to the daybed by the window. Plops the book back in her lap.

The daughter pulls up a stool to the phone. Opens her daybook to Tuesday.

Bath, she writes in red pen.

Lunch.

Homecare.

Bath.

Bath.

Bath.

Bath.

Bath.

Bath.

HOME ALARM

Noise and more noise next door, all night long. Banging. Music. Loud cooking sounds. Sex noises. The lot. I flip the pillow to the cool side. Hear the ceiling fan hum. Relax a little. Then a bang or a sex noise. Awful.

I get up, walk around the house. I'm a new widow. Bereaved, recently. I buy too much food. I don't watch television. He always had the clicker; I forget that I can watch what I want now. I never refused him in bed. Even if we weren't speaking. But I wouldn't put it in my mouth. He bathed once a week. For church. His side of the bed still smells. I like the extra space, in bed. I'd sleep like a baby. If not for the banging and sex noises.

I think of what to yell out the window. I'm not a yeller. The both of them, next door, the both of them look tough.

Her punched-in nose, the ankle bracelet I hear tinkle down the driveway. His gotchies on the laundry line. Big as a table cloth. I lie down again.

My own peach jam on toast. Apple juice. All my pills in my pill teacup. The paper, folded so it's just the funnies, so Dear Abby is where I can't see her.

Slappy the Cow in a heap. Mud all over her tummy. I'm an udder mess! says the balloon above her head.

I feel hot. I slip out of my housecoat. I feel cold.

My son at the door. It's not even nine. Through the glass I see a McDonald's bag. He's 41. I let him in. I've got a stomach ache, he says. But I'm hungry as shit.

He pulls off the runners I bought him. No socks.

My sink doesn't work. I think it's full of hair, he says.

Donny, I say. Put your shoes on the shoe mat there. Please.

The dog comes out to see who it is. Sees who it is. Goes back into the bathroom. It likes to lie in there. Face pressed against the cold toilet.

He sits at the table and empties his bag. Two Egg McMuffins. I watch him eat with his mouth open. My only child. I had three miscarriages.

I think you're doing something wrong, said my husband.

What am I doing wrong? I said back.

Some kind of I-don't-know-what. Sabotage. Boiling hot baths. Or — do you punch yourself?

Yes, I said. I punch myself. I couldn't even sit through *Jaws*. You think I'm going to go around knocking myself in the guts?

Who knows? he said. Who even knows?

Donny wipes his hands on his shirt.

I got an eye appointment, he says. At ten. You need to come to it.

Why do I need to come?

It's a big deal. I can't see right. I want to make sure he doesn't pull a fast one.

Who is it?

Brinkley.

I look at my pot and pan rack. Donny, Dr. Brinkley is nearly eighty. What kind of fast one is he going to pull?

He wiggles his brow.

He might put drops in my eyes. Then go for the arse.

I'll be right back, I say.

I go where my phone books are. Look up the thing I'm going to get.

I can't go with you, I say to my son. I have to make a phone call.

For what?

An alarm of some kind. A home alarm.

Like what kind?

The kind that keeps creeps away.

He clucks his tongue. Think you're gonna get raped? Who's gonna rape you? Nobody'd want to rape you.

I'm getting older. It's a good thing to have.

I don't have one.

You're a three-hundred-pound man.

Please come with me to the eye thing. I'm scared. I'll drive you to the alarm store if you go with me. As long as the alarm store isn't hundreds of miles away.

It's not a store, I say. I have to call them.

Donny blinks. Rubs his eyes with his fat fists.

Fine. I say. Fine.

Which looks more clear and crisp, the doctor says. This one? Or this one?

Dr. Brinkley's making things click on the eye machine.

Neither, Donny says. No. The first one.

The room is dark. By the light of the desk lamp I flip through an old People. An actress whose name I don't know says breast cancer was the best thing that ever happened to her.

The doctor keeps clicking but looks at me.

Remember when you brought poor Lindy in, years ago? he says.

Lindy? I say. Who's that?

Aren't you Joan Clark?

Joan Clark is my sister-in-law. She passed away. I'm Carol Clark.

Poor Joan. Threw up in her sleep and choked on it. Dead. A lot of people are dead.

Carol, the doctor says. Yes. How is your vision these days?

Donny needs bi-focals.

Mum, he says in the car, what if I don't just need bi-focals? What if I'm going all-the-way blind?

The doctor would've said so, I say.

But he couldn't even remember you from Auntie Joan. He could've fucked up.

Don't worry, Donny, I say. You're not going blind. There'll be plenty of time to go blind down the road.

I call the alarm place. The girl says a lot of stuff I don't listen to. I buy what she says to buy. They're coming tomorrow.

I don't sleep. Sounds like a party tonight, next door. On their deck.

That's nothing, I hear the tough woman say to whoever. I went to work with cum in my hair and didn't notice 'til lunchtime!

Everybody laughs.

I close my eyes. Imagine the alarm installation man. Handsome. Thoughtful. So patient with me.

RAPE AND KILL

Lynn is late for work. She runs up the stairs.

Hi Lynn, Beth says, watering can in her hand. Your hair looks nice today.

She points at Lynn's thin hair. Are you wearing makeup? says Beth.

A little, says Lynn. I had my colours done for free. She said I was a winter. I hate winter.

Beth nods and walks to her cubicle. Lynn watches her walk. She once asked Beth out for Chinese food after work. It was windy and Beth didn't hear her and walked away. Or Beth did hear but walked away anyway.

Lynn sees so much of herself in Beth. That time that Beth was singing to the song on the little radio? And Lynn joined in on the chorus? And Beth stopped singing? Lynn has tried to be Beth's friend, even her best friend. Tried and tried. Lynn always gives her all. But people, Beth and people, they don't seem to see that in Lynn.

Jeanne is late, too. She brings in pastries. Strudel, black iced cupcakes. Lynn takes a cupcake and clinks it to Jeanne's cupcake, like wine glasses. Lynn takes a big bite of cupcake. Breaks a tooth. Swallows. Looks around.

A meeting after lunch.

We've had complaints, says the boss. Seems we're hanging up on customers.

I never do.

Neither do I.

I've only ever done that once. And that was that awful man who said he wanted to drown me in you-know-what.

It's never appropriate to hang up on a customer, says the boss. I don't care if they say they're gonna rape and kill you. They say, I'm gonna rape and kill you — you say, great! Can't wait!

The room is silent.

I agree, says Lynn. All customer contact is precious. All human contact. We should always just sit there and take it. I never did hang up on anyone. Not in my personal or my at work time.

Well said, says the boss.

Lynn starts to write on her notepad. Jeanne and Beth both look at her pad. She cups her hand around it. Hides what she's writing: *Lynn Lynn Olivia Newton-John Best wishes, Olivia Newton-John Lynn Lynn Lynn*

Beth keeps running to the bathroom. Lynn looks at the mouthpiece on Beth's headset. Foamy spit.

Jeanne dumps the day's last pot of coffee. A man comes for Beth. In overalls and rubber boots. Tattoo at his wrist. *E Z BREEZEE*. Balloon letters. He takes Beth's purse. Hangs it from his own, brown shoulder.

Are you alright, Beth? says Jeanne.

It's that damn fertility drug. Last night my heart raced 'til I thought it would stop altogether.

Jeanne puts her hand on the man's back.

You take care of her, Jeanne says to him. That would be tough luck, if her heart stopped.

Don't you worry, the man says. I can start it up again.

Beth and the man walk out slowly. Her head against his chest. Jeanne smiles. Looks at Lynn. Frowns.

Who was that? says Lynn.

That's Beth's friend.

Oh. Right.

Lynn walks to her purse. Stops. Walks back to Jeanne.

Gosh I hope it's not worse than she thinks, says Lynn.

What is? says Jeanne.

Her feeling sick. I hope it's only her pregnant drugs.

It is.

It might not be. It might be — who knows? AIDS.

AIDS? Why on earth —

Now I'm worried that Beth could have AIDS. I can smell it.

That is the sickest thing I've ever heard.

Right. And she's the sickest thing I ever smelled. I'm scared.

You're an idiot. You're a fucking idiot. You can't smell AIDS.

On her you can.

You should be institutionalized. I —

Jeanne looks up. Looks down.

And what does AIDS smell like, exactly? Jeanne says.

Like you. You be nice to me, Jeanne.

This is just beyond the pale. You're sick. I'm leaving.

Jeanne leaves. Comes back for her pansy print thermos. Leaves again.

Lynn eats cold toast at her card table. Her housecoat buttoned up to the neck. The phone rings.

Hello?

Is this Lynn?

This is Lynn.

It's Beth.

Beth! I was just thinking —

Listen. You fucking loser bitch. I don't have AIDS.

Oh! I'm so glad.

So don't go telling my friends and co-workers that I'm a fucking AIDS victim. Some of us have lives. Some of us don't live in La-La Land. Got it?

Beth. It's just. I care about how you're doing.

Well, don't. Ugh. AIDS. Do you even know anyone with AIDS?

Actually, yes. Mr. Scott's son. With those awful things on his face.

That's impetigo. And he's retarded anyway. Where's he gonna get AIDS?

Oh. Umm. How's your —

Just don't talk about me. Or to me. Ever. Okay?

Okay. I'm so sorry. See you tomorrow.

Beth hangs up on Lynn. Lynn holds her phone for awhile, away from her face. In both hands. Like a bat.

Late night. Lynn goes for a walk.

She comes to an intersection. Breathes deeply, shifts foot to foot. Waits for the walk sign. A woman stops beside her. Looks Lynn up and down.

Umm. Excuse me, the woman says.

Yes? says Lynn.

You're bleeding all down your legs.

I am? Oh. I am.

Guess you had a bit of an accident.

The woman walks with her, across the street.

It's absolutely nothing to be ashamed of. I got it all over my wedding dress.

Lynn stops in the middle of the road. So does the woman. A pick-up idles. A white-haired man sticks his head out his window. Looks at the woman. The woman looks back at him. They both look at Lynn, and her short, bloody legs. Yellow light. Red.

IN PLUM

My husband. His hair is long now. To his elbows. When he comes out of the shower, he has it all twisted and pulled to one side.

He threw up. On the kitchen floor. A brown and red puddle on our white tile. Our cat, Cluckie, tried to lick it up. I picked her up and threw her into the dining room.

Yesterday he went out to mow the lawn. I sat at my loom. I didn't hear the mower. Didn't hear it. Didn't hear it. I rolled my eyes and said *now what?* even though I was all alone. Except for Cluckie.

I went out and he was sitting at our picnic table, head between his knees. Hair grazing the grass.

I asked him if he was alright.

Oh yeah, he said. Just having a moment.

Now he's thrown up. I go under the sink and look in my rag bag. Find an old T-shirt. The one I got at the Heart concert we went to, the summer I miscarried.

I rip it in half. I wipe it up. His vomit. Cluckie comes around again. Fuck off, Cluckie!

I take out steaks to thaw.

It starts to rain. I see our neighbour, the man, run inside, laughing. Stops raining.

I want to put a dress on for dinner. I go to the bedroom. He's lying in there in the dark.

I just need to turn on the light for a sec, sweetie, I say.

Oh, please don't, he says. Sweetie. I feel really off. I just need the dark for a bit.

I run my hands across my part of the closet. I feel velour, felt, spandex. I pick something cotton and walk into the hall with it.

A housecoat.

Supper's on the go. I sit in my housecoat at the kitchen table, putting on nail polish. Plum.

My nails aren't nice. They're warped. One of them, the pinkie, got caught in a car door and now it's like a little bowl. My pinkie nail can hold a drop of water in the middle of it.

They're nice with nail polish on them. He likes them painted. One time, in Duluth, he took my hands in his. He looked at my nails all done up in plum. Looked at them like they were behind glass, in a museum.

With those nails, he said, you could just shoot me in the head and I'd love it. Just to see those nails on a gun.

That time was also close to the time we conceived our miscarriage.

I call to my husband.

Supper's ready.

Supper.

Honey. Supper.

He moans. I hear the bed creak.

Gee whiz, honey, he says. I still feel off. I'm just gonna lay here for a bit. Maybe put mine in the fridge.

I go into the hallway and close the bedroom door.

I turn on the radio by the microwave while the crusty buns warm up. It's *Songs of the Ukraine*. I turn it off.

I cut up his steak in tiny pieces. Put the plate on the floor. Cluckie comes running.

The sun sets. I eat my supper on the porch.

There's nothing on TV. I leave the front door unlocked and walk to the video store.

A woman is yelling at the video store girl.

I can't have a late charge, she says, because I never rented what you say I rented. I mean, I *hate* Meryl Streep. Fuck that bitch! If you charge me for it I can't even say what I'll do.

I squeeze past her. The new release aisle is all picked over.

Beside the classics section is the adult section. There's a man there with his little girl.

How come everyone just doesn't have hair down to the floor? she says to her dad.

Split My Slit. Granny's Ass. The Cum Diet. I move sideways to the man and the girl.

There's so much selection, I say.

I'm just looking, the man says.

I've never watched pornography, I say. I guess it could
be quite — a journey.

I don't know, he says. Lacey, take your hair out of your
fuckin' mouth.

He takes the girl by the arm and slides past me. I watch
them walk out.

There's one movie with a title in blue glitter. I pick it up.

Love Explosion. I tilt the case to catch the light. Real spar-
kles.

I put it back.

ANCHORED IN HOPE

First day of school. All of them tanned and mosquito bit. I
pull at my bangs, try to hide my smooth pale forehead. Fold
my arms and legs. Face front.

I'm Mrs.Binns, she says, beside her name in pink chalk.
Let's get to know each other. My first name is Helen. You're
my very first grade six class. My very first class, period! I
like riding my bike, and I love watermelon! I also love music, and music is how I'm going to get know each and every
one of you!

We're each to bring in our favourite record. The one that
says who we are.

Who is Jamie? she says, reading her attendance list. Who
is Teresa? Who is Akiko?

But first, who is Tim Abraham, whose name is first on
her list? My last name starts with a T. So I have time to de-
cide who I am.

Mother is on the ottoman.

Oh that meat, Mother says. Did the meat affect you? Do you feel altered somehow?

By the hamburger? I say.

I feel altered. Somehow. I fear that I'm past the point of consuming anything, ever. And then what? Enlightenment? Or just this feeling, and then starvation, and then, of course, death?

Go to bed, Mother.

Father's in the basement. Shirtless. Lifting homemade weights. Buckets of bird seed hanging from a broken broom. He's nearly 70.

I sit at the top of the steps. Watch the old tattoo stretch across his muscle. An anchor. *Anchored in Hope* underneath it. I feel his heartbeat in my teeth.

Is that hard to do? I say.

Eight...Nine...Ten. He drops the weights. Wipes his face with a yellowed undershirt.

Do you need some water, Father?

No. I'm used to lifting weights. You should take it up, fatty.

Akiko brings in Kenny Rogers.

That was so rousing! says Mrs.Binns. Does anyone know what 'rousing' means?

I know. But I look out the window.

When something is rousing, she says, it's invigorating. And what is invigorating? Firecrackers! Tidal waves! I could go on and on and on.

I go through his rack of records in the basement. Covers warped and musty.

Between Vera Lynn and Acker Bilk is a magazine, swollen a bit by the damp. *Milky and Loving It!* Page after page of laughing women, squirting milk from their breasts. Onto red walls. Into their own mouths. I stick it back where it was. I take the last record in the rack, don't even look at what I've picked.

Mrs. Binns in a yellow T-shirt and corduroy skirt to the floor. She walks slowly to the stereo. Holds my record like it's a lit birthday cake.

She puts the record on. It skips. She lifts the needle. Sets it down a little further in. Skips. She takes the record off.

Isn't this disappointing, she says. Isn't this just a heart-break. Did I not insist that you play the record at home first, to prevent this very situation? Yes. I did.

I did play it, I lie.

Now we'll never get to know this unique piece of music. And it is unique. I have it at home.

Maybe you could bring yours in, I say.

She tilts her head sideways, so her dangly dove earring rests against her face. Boundary crossed! This is not about me. This is not about what I have or do not have at home, she says.

She walks to her desk. Stops. Turns.

How. Dare. You. She says. How even dare you?

I walk home with the record. Mother in a lawn chair in the middle of the lawn.

I've stepped into the sun, she says. And now I'm sitting in it. I know I won't be incinerated. And if I am? Hooray!

Dad in the kitchen. Dress shirt, no pants. Cutting onions for a sandwich.

Whatcha doing with my Jim Reeves record?

I had to bring in a record I liked.

Since when did you like Jim Reeves, freako?

I don't know. I don't know what I like. So I picked something you like. But it's scratched.

Scratched? Give it here.

He takes the record, pulls it from the sleeve. Eyes the grooves.

Just dusty. Go get that oil, that special oil I've got.

I go get the special oil. In the hall closet, third shelf, with all our feather dusters.

Then, you just wipe with the groove, he says. His hand goes 'round and 'round.

Here. Dollar to a donut, it plays like a charm. Let's throw it on. He goes into the living room, in his white dress shirt and black socks. Dancing a little. Like the record's already started.

Now Mother's in the house, in her chair. Starts giggling and rocking back and forth. Dad shimmies.

Take a picture of me! Mother yells.

I wait for the music.

C'mere n' take our picture, my father calls to me. My mother on the loveseat. Blanket across her lap. My father behind her. His hands on her shoulders.

We don't have a camera, I say.

Take a picture! Mother is screaming now.
Just press the button, Father says.
The flash will scald me, my mother says.
It's daytime, Father says. No flash.
My mother shuts her eyes tight. Father smiles like he's lifting weights. I press the button.

BLUE GLASS

Dan is watching Bill shave. Bill shaves against the grain of his beard. Blood beads. White foam sideburns. Bill singing falsetto.

You're doing it wrong, Dan says.

I know how to shave. I have thick growth. I have to be aggressive with it.

You don't have thick growth, Dan says. I have thick growth. You're downy. She-male.

Go away, says Bill. I feel good today.

I'm sorry. You do have thick growth. We both do. I've noticed that.

Dan goes and stands in the foyer. He looks at Bill's paint-
ings. His Fake Saint Series. A bug-eyed nun in a lake of pee.
A smiling nun hoisting a dumbbell.

He thinks of his old place. The stained wallpaper.

Dan goes back to the bathroom. Can I make us a nice
breakfast? he says. Bill's cell goes off. Bill's cell, clipped to
the towel wrapped around his waist.

Hello? Rod? Bill says. Your voice is so faint. What? Oh
God. That's so awful.

No. Oosh. Did they do a scan? And? Praise be, I guess.
Are you at home? Who's with you?

Bill wanders into the kitchen on his cell. Dan follows him.
He looks at Bill's big bare back. Muscle by muscle. Bill's hand
in a fist, knuckles knocking on the cutting board. The blue
glass bowl there.

Bill starts to rock as he talks. Don't even worry about it,
he says into his cell, rocking back. He loses balance. His hand
slides across the island. The blue glass bowl goes flying.
Knocks against the fridge. Shatters on the floor. A big shard
in the cat dish.

Shit, says Bill. I've gotta go, sweetie. I'll be right over.
Bill bends down to fish the shard from the cat dish. Poor
Rod, Bill says. He fell off his roof. Cracked his head open.
Big concussion.

Who's Rod? says Dan.

From my group.

Which group?

The artists' therapy group. And he was in the group show I did last summer. His doctor says he's surprised he's not dead or paralyzed.

Dan sees how Bill's bare foot nudges a piece of blue glass.

I really loved that bowl, Bill.

Sorry.

You gave me that bowl.

Sorry, says Bill. I was upset about Rod.

Who I've never even heard of.

You have. You've met him. He said you looked robust and you thought he meant fat.

Is Rod that AIDS one who makes an ugly doll everytime he gets a rash?

No. That's Kevin. Why are you always so severe?

I'm sorry. Really. I'm sorry Rod cracked his head open. I'll go get a dustpan for the glass.

In the basement Dan finds the dustpan, on top of a box. The box says 'old winter clothes', in his writing.

He lifts the flaps and dips his hand in. Silk and velvet. Slick rope. He tugs it. A tassel. Not his clothes. His old clothes are fat clothes. Flannel everything.

Upstairs, Dan holds the cape like a matador.

What's this? Dan says.

Bill on his way out the door.

My robe! Where was it?

In the basement.

Oh. Huh. I thought Marty had it.

Dan starts to say, who's Marty? but stops himself. Bill takes his keys from the key dish.

Why do you have a velvet cape?

Sometimes we role play. It goes deep. It's cathartic.

Who do you play with?

Artist friends. Assorted artists. Marty, Rod. Kevin when he's up to it. We role play, walk around, partake of a *derive*, in a casual way.

Dan sucks breath. Shakes his head.

What's a *derive*?

I totally have to go, says Bill.

Dan on the porch. Two butterflies flutter over the pansy basket.

Don't forget your faggot *derive* cape! Dan calls down the sidewalk. He throws the cape. It lands on the porch railing. Flutters.

A girl walks past. She stops when she sees the red velvet.

Is that yours? the girl says.

No. It's my friend's, Dan says.

Oh yeah. Can I try it on?

Dan looks at the cape. The tassles sparkle in the sun.

No.

You try it on then, the girl says.

Dan smiles at the girl. He picks it up and throws it around himself.

How does it look? says Dan.

Nice, says the girl.

Do I look tubby in it?

A little.

The girl keeps walking. Dan takes off the cape. Folds it neatly into a square. Brings it inside. The cape is musty. He throws it in the laundry hamper.

Fine fabric. He takes it out of the hamper and puts it in with dry cleaning. Rumpled suits. Bill's special cape.

TWICE

The couple brings the blanket ends together. A scent of cut lawn.

I can't wait to sleep with this tonight, the woman says.

Me too, says the man. I love fresh things.

They kiss over the toaster. He takes a big breath. His asthma has gone away. His last attack was before they met. He was sitting on the end of his bed, looking at his hand.

And he had an attack. That was before. His hair was longer. He had a cat.

Doing things. Half her foot in his mouth. She watches him. He looks up from her foot.

I'm just boiling, she says.

Erotically, he says, mouth full, or is it hot in here?

I'm spinning, she says. Yes. I love our house.

Two new bathrobes folded on the daybed.

Her jewelry box. With the tricky clasp. She goes through her jewelry. Box in her lap. Her nanna's brooch. Her nanna's ring. The new pearls. Her first pearls. Her pink pearls. She runs a finger over where she keeps her solitaire. From her mom, when she got all 90s in her last year of dental school. Her dead mom. Her solitaire. Gone. Where is her solitaire?

She wanders through their new home. The furniture — all his. She had so little coming in to it. She had crates for end tables. Empty cupboards. All her friends work friends. She barely needed a phone. But she had one. It's in their new garage now.

A woman knocking at the door.

Hi there, says the woman, holding a pie. Did I wake you? It's afternoon. But you might work shift work. Do you work shift work?

No. No, I don't.

I'm not a psycho, says the pie woman. I don't welcome people usually. I love your drapes. Pier One?

The — Oh. Yes, I think so.

Nice. Pier One drapes to peer through! Anyway. I see you two leave the house together. Smiling. It's nice. Refreshing. The one on the other side of me — I saw her eat out of my garbage. Twice. Anyway. Welcome!

The pie. Mincemeat. Still hot.

His hard-on starts when he fastens his seatbelt. It gets bigger with things he sees. Leaning tree. Lemonade stand. Old woman, waiting to cross.

A girl in the car stopped next to his. She blows smoke out her window. Into his face. He smiles.

She rocks in his walnut rocker. Rocks and rocks. Her nylons crease at the toes. If he took her solitaire, was it for a keep-sake? Or is he a thief? The kind allergic to grace and tender-ness? Will she wake up, one night, with their new knife to her throat?

She hears his car pull up. The pop of tire on gravel. This sound makes her jump up and run. Down the hall, to the end of the empty bedroom. Back again, to the front door. Back and forth she runs. Glides, in nylons. When he opens the door she slides into him and his hard-on. He drops his briefcase on her big toe. They both gasp.

BABYSIT

My coffee pot. Keeps coffee hot. I paid an arm and a leg for it. I click my nails against it. Then I pour a cup for me. And a cup for Deb. Or Sally. I forget. The girl in the living room.

My son is on his blanket. The fringe. It looks dirty. When the girl goes, I'll cut it all off.

So! Kate says you're just the bee's knees, I say, handing her a cup. She says you're indispensable.

She looks at my antique tin goose and its tin goslings.

Who's Kate? she says. Oh. Right. She lives right nearby. I like her baby. He sleeps a lot. That birthmark on his poor face.

Her big breasts, straining the Cotton Ginny sweatshirt. She'd make a good wet nurse.

So it'll just be Wednesdays, I say. Ten to four. I'm sure

it'll be great. Let's look around the house. It's pretty much baby-proofed. Of course, that doesn't stop me from tripping over things. I'm so klutzy. Eight years of ballet! I cross my legs and there's a body count!

I show her the bathroom. The hall. My son's room. My room. The pillow at the foot of the bed. I brought a man home last night. He knew me from parties. Shaved my bush down, bald. I try not to scratch in front of Deb? Sandra?

You're versed with basic baby care, then? I say to her in the hall.

Sure. I took that course with the Red Cross. So.

She steps back.

And. What if he started to choke? I ask her.

I lay him on my knee.

And?

I'd punch him on the back. Well. Not punch, but.

Perfect. Excuse me for just a second.

I go in the bathroom. Turn the fan on. Open the window. Light up a joint. Smoke it fast, sitting on the toilet lid. I flick the roach through a hole in the window screen.

She's in the kitchen.

How about, I say, how about I take a nice picture of you and my little one?

She touches her hair.

My hair is so. But, yeah. Okay.

I open up my camera cupboard. It sits beside the salt box. The dusty lens. I should take more pictures, more often.

Should I pick him up? she says.

Yes. No. Maybe just lean over him.

She leans. The crack of her cleavage.

Nice blanket, she says.

You think so? I say. I hate it. I just hate it. What possessed me? I can't even stand it. I want to burn it. Smile!

The flash. The baby sneezes. I put the camera back in its cupboard.

Actually, I say, I was just about to bathe him. Wanna help?

She looks to the left. To the right.

I'm kinda supposed to get the car back to my mom.

Hmm. I kind of insist on observing your baby bathing skills.

She bites her lip. I pick up my son. She follows me into the bathroom.

I watch her fill the baby tub and put it on the little table. Closes the window to keep in the heat. Tests the water with her hand. Again and again.

She unbuttons his pajamas. He's nice and still. Such a good baby.

She slowly lowers him into the water. He starts to scream. Splash.

It's okay! It's okay! we both say.

Her top is getting wet.

Your top is getting wet, I say. Let's really get in the trenches!

I unbutton my blouse and slip out of it. Drop it in the

sink. Much better. I'd always be nude if I could. I met my boy's father nude. In a club. My cold beer was pressed to my chest, leaving dew there.

I give her the eyeball. Serious business. I hold the baby in the tub. She pulls off her sweatshirt. Barrettes snag on it. It finally comes off.

There we go! I say. Liberty! Now let's clean some baby!

FLORA

Storm is coming definitely definitely, Mommy says. Standing at the window. Long grey hair to her knees. Bare feet. The sparrow tattoo on her ankle.

Daddy puts down the broken toaster. Goes to the window. Puts his skinny arm around her shoulder.

Where? It's the sunniest day ever, sweetheart! he says.

I can feel it. I feel clairvoyant today. This morning I thought of Cher. And then she was on the radio.

Wow, Daddy says.

Try me. Ask me something, Mommy says.

Daddy looks at the red dent in Mommy's forehead. From when she hit the TV table doing yoga. Healing nice. He rolls his eyes. Mom fingers the crease in her forehead.

Flora's going to call! She announces.

Flora? Daddy says. Who on earth is Flora?

I don't know. Flora's going to call and our lives will never be the same.

Daddy laughs.

Toilet flush. Granny comes out of the bathroom. When you said you were doing the bathroom in black, Granny says, I had to wonder. But it's real nice. Relaxing. I dozed off. Set me up a cot in the bathtub!

Mommy, Daddy says, Trisha says she feels psychic today.

Oh yeah? Granny says. Doorbell. I get it.

A skinny lady I've never seen before.

Hi! she says. My name is Frienda. Is your mother or father at home?

We're right here, Mommy and Daddy say. They come to the door.

Hi! she says. My name is Frienda. I'm from the Love Brigade. I'm getting to know my neighbours. Hi there!

Hi there, says Daddy. Where do you live? Are you in the old Johnson house?

No, says Frienda. I'm from Winnipeg.

That's two hundred miles away, says Mommy. That's not really in our neighbourhood.

I like to think that everyone is my neighbour. Have you heard about the Love Brigade? It's too exciting!

No, says Daddy, I don't really think —

The Love Brigade, says Frienda, is an offshoot of the more well-known Faith Brigade. We were founded in —

Granny barrels to the door.

You were founded in shit! Granny says. Get lost!

She slams the door shut.

Daddy makes dinner. We eat it.

We go in the living room. Mommy does her learner's yoga. We watch TV.

Close to my bedtime. Mommy sits with us, towel on her head. Nobody says things.

I'm not a cranky woman, Granny says.

Daddy puts the TV on mute.

People like that just put me right off, she says, looking down. When I was a girl, she says, before I was married, I got mixed up in one of those cult kind of things. I've never spoken of it. I —

Daddy puts his hand up.

Mommy, he says, you don't have to explain. Faith is important, no matter how you come by it.

Just let me talk, Granny says. I was lonely at the time. Didn't think I'd ever find someone. My cleft palate and all that. Then I fell in with this group. And they were all peace and love and good feelings.

Granny puts her head in her hands.

And then — Oh Christ! she says, starting to cry. And then they made me — Oh Christ! — they made me put my mouth on a lady's asshole and move it around. My mouth! Jesus. Oh Christ!

Granny cries and cries.

Go to bed! Right this minute! Mommy says. Her turban, coming undone.

THE SPELL

All the lights, all the lamps go out. I look out the window.
Streetlights out, too.

Shit, says Max.

I know, I say.

I hear his walker scrape the floor. I sit and look at the
dark. Lights come back.

I open my book again. *Candle Magic!* I'm skimming it.
*The Deeper Love Spell. The Health and Well Being Spell. The Safe
Travel Spell.* The government garnisheed my last pay for back
taxes. I'm looking for *The Fuck Off, I'm Poor and My Boyfriend's
a Crip Spell.*

There's one for abundance. On the abundance page someone has written *that'll be the day* in pen. The book is a library
cast-off. I set it down on the coffee table. Carefully. Like it's
a wizard book.

Zellers. In the candle aisle is a woman my age. She stands beside me. There's just too much selection, she says. Holds her head, like selection makes her dizzy.

I tiptoe for pink. Squat for red. Then I get the hell away from her.

At home Max is peeling turnip for dinner. Sometimes I put things just out of his reach. He's a recent crip. I like to see the grit and hope in his face when he walkers to the thing I put just out of reach. One day the hope will turn to hate. That could also be something.

He peels. Smiles as I walk through the kitchen. With my candle book. And my candles. I close the bedroom door. Lock it.

A blue candle. I light it.

Dear magical universe, I say. Tell me all about what I need to know about — I look at the back of the matchbook. It says *Rape is Rape. Period.* I blow out my candle. March into the kitchen.

Where did this come from? I say, waving the matchbook in his face.

I don't know, he says.

Have you been snooping around women's shelters?

He drops the peeler in the sink.

Yah. Yes. I've been snooping around women's shelters. Christ.

It's possible. I could see it. I could see you snooping around a shelter in your walker. Trying to sniff out some grateful, battered puss.

He holds the turnip like a mic.

I don't like this joke.

It's not a joke. I'm serious. Like. Nuremberg serious. Mister Turnip Peeler.

I go outside. To the garage. I don't know why.

There's a big plastic doll by the tires. Real yellow hair. I don't know where it came from. I hate dolls. I played with sticks when I was little.

A can of turpentine on the workbench. I never come in here. Dolls. Turpentine. It's all a mystery to me.

I spill some of the turpentine into a dirty doily. Put to my face and breathe deep. Don't feel much. Then feel thick and packed. Like I live in a mattress.

Max walkers in.

What are you doing? he says.

Huffing solvents.

Fuck. How long have you been doing this?

Like, a minute.

I mean, in the scheme of things.

I just started. Try it.

I'm making supper.

So? Just one huff. One huff, for me.

No.

A lot of famous people huff things. It's something to do. Just once.

I pour a big helping for him. He barely sniffs. He sniffs like a faggot.

Don't sniff like a faggot, I say. Really sniff. Really huff.

He grinds his face into the cloth. Sniffs it up. He sways.

I smile. He smiles. All around him, dust particles sparkle. Magic.

FRANK AND TRUDY

Trudy goes over to Frank's house. She brings brownies and *Field & Stream*.

The road to Frank's is bumpy. He says How'd ya make out? She says When? Where?

She bends over the kitchen counter and he screws her fast. Frank says 'and' with every pump. Trudy says 'ho.' And ho. And ho. And ho.

Trudy goes home, back down the bumpy road. Frank sits on a couch. Lights a cigarette. Tries to remember when he went from regular to menthol. '67? '68?

Frank is 81. All the furniture is new. One chair, the brown one, hasn't even been sat on. Frank sits on it.

He gets up and takes a steak out of the freezer. Wonders about a beer, or a big glass of buttermilk.

In bed Frank reads the note he almost sent to Trudy, the day after they met. The day before he first screwed her, front and backdoor.

Dear Trudy,

I saw a girl on TV with the same shirt as you. That made me think of you and your shirt. And what might be under that shirt! It was sure nice to meet you the other day.

You don't know this, but I've been impotent since well before my wife died.

Since I was 36, actually. I've had a real problem with that. I thought it was all over, for good. But then guess what happened after I met you? I want to thank you a lot for everything. It's a bit of a miracle. I guess you're something special. I sure wouldn't mind having you over. I'm getting the Rug Doctor and scrubbing the rugs tomorrow morning. So anytime after that.

Sincerely,

Frank

He crumples it up. He's glad he didn't send it. There's no point to that kind of courtship runaround anymore.

Trudy lives with her mother. Trudy can't read.

*

Frank orders a coffee at Zellers. New waitress. White hair. Button-up sweater overtop her uniform.

Would you like pie? says the waitress.

What kind? says Frank.

Raisin.

Oh. No. Thank you. I hate raisins.

So do I! Rat turds. You want some rat turd pie? I sure don't!

Frank takes his pack of smokes from a shirt pocket. His nipple is hard. He juts his chest out a little.

How're ya makin' out here? he says.

Great. It's like a family. I've got awful edema. My ankles are just like blood sausages. So Ann takes the plates to the table for me.

She can use the exercise with the ass on her. You want to go out tonight?

Gee whiz. I don't even know your name!

The other girls here all know me. Ask one of 'em.

She walks over to the other waitress. Pulls her away from a table of three. They whisper, cupping each other's ears. She walks back to Frank.

Frank, she says.

Maybe, he says.

Well. I haven't gone out for so long.

What's that?

I say I haven't gone out for so long.

Huh. 'cause of the edema?

No. This and that and the other thing.

Oh. Knocked up, eh?

No! Oh! she says. Oh Frank!

*

Frank drives around. Three burnt down houses, side by side by side. Smells like cookies baking. He rolls down the window.

A cat bolts out from under a burnt porch. Runs across the road. Frank brakes hard. The street is empty. The cats runs into a flower bed. Red peonies shake.

He drives slow, pulls into a parking lot. The engine is his heart, still pounding. Two girls are at the other end of the lot. It looks like they're dancing. Frank squints. The girls are stomping. Smiling and stomping on a squirrel.

He unzips his dress pants. Fishes for his limp cock. Pulls it out and pumps it a bit. Puts it back in. The town office clock gongs twice.

Frank drives home. Sits in the new brown chair. Checks the time. He's picking up the waitress at six.

*

She walks past him at the mall doors. Fast. She makes wind with her walk. His thin yellow hair flutters.

Hey! he says. Hey there!

She stops. Her fat back to him.

Here I am right here, he says.

She turns sideways. He sees her goiter scar. It's a gray chain across her neck.

I see you, she says. I see you and you just make me sick.

Why's that? he says.

I don't talk to old buggers who fuck retarded girls. Awful. Awful! Does she even know she's getting fucked? I bet she doesn't. I bet she thinks she sat on a broom or something. Awful. Well. I'm not retarded. So I guess you're outta luck.

She's not retarded. She's just brain damaged. And a real nice person, he says.

The waitress walks away. Gets into a car with the other waitresses. The ones in the back all bounce and squeeze together to make room.

Frank shakes his little yellow head.

*

When he gets home he calls Trudy. Her mother answers.

Luh, says Trudy's mother.

Chocolate! Chocolate! Frank hears Trudy say in the background, her voice circular, like she's running through the house.

It's Frank, says Frank. Is Trudy there?

Nuh. Just me, says the mother.

But I can hear her.

TV. Just me here.

Oh. Okay.

I'm lonely, says the mother. Just like I'm crazy. You can go to bed with me if you want.

What's that? says Frank.

The mother screams Trudy's name.

Here comes Trudy, she says.

Frank hangs up. Thinks about lighting a smoke.

I TURN DEVIL

Mine smokes like two big packs a day. How much does yours smoke?

About that. Player's Light.

Mine, too! Player's Light.

My dad smokes, too. But Gord's dad is dead so I don't say so. Got cut in half by a semi on the highway. It was in the paper. He got semi-detached, my dad says, smoking.

Gord is my friend. Right now, my only friend. I used to have five friends. One moved down east, one went to bible camp, one went mean and said I lived in a trailer which I don't, one I don't like anymore. I'm forgetting one. I guess that's why I don't have that friend. Gord is my only friend.

I met him at swimming lessons. We both kind of have boy boobs. We both jumped from the dock with arms wrapped around our fronts.

Gord and me say we'll meet tonight. Then we walk away from each other, through the charred field.

Panties on the coffee table. Mom and Dad are doing their thing in the big bedroom. They don't hug or kiss in front of me. Or say things to each other. They say things out loud. To themselves. Last night, during supper, Mom said her hysterectomy made her feel like some sort of sexy robot. Then dessert, and Dad said my great-granddad got a girl pregnant at ninety. I did the dishes.

You like my little brown-eye, don't you, I hear Mom say in the big bedroom.

What a wet one you are, I hear Dad say.

It's sunset in the charred field.

You ever play Devil-Angel? Gord says.

No. What's that?

It's where the one person plays the devil, then drives the angel crazy with evil 'til the angel turns into a devil.

Do you have to wear costumes?

I'll be the devil.

He throws me in a scorpion pit of blackened wheat. The wind is killer lava. God is a lezbo, he says, a lezbo that eats babies. I turn devil. Night and mosquitoes. We're both hungry.

I follow him down his end of the field.

His mother on the porch, smoking.

You the Laurence's kid? she says.

I nod.

Your mom still work at the bank?

Yeah. She had a leave of absence for surgery. But she's going back soon.

Huh. She's a toughie, eh? I know people she's made cry over loans and that.

She had surgery, I say. But she's feeling better.

I go with Gord to the side door. Don't go crazy in there, his mother yells.

We angle past bits of jagged awning to get to the rec room. Gord sits down on an old brown couch. He takes off his shirt. His boy boobs.

Where's the brassiere? I say. I don't know why I say it.

Fuck you! he screams. Why did you say that? You're just as bad. Worse!

I sit down. He gets up. Hands on hips. Huffing and puffing. I tell him I'm sorry. He sits back down.

I want you to feel something, he says.

He puts my hand on the back of his neck. A lump.

That's nothing, I say.

But it hurts, he says.

Maybe it's a bite.

From what? A black widow?

Don't worry about it. Things like that just come and go.

I take my hand away. His back to me. I take my hands, reach around, cup a boob each.

Why are you doing that? he says. Not angry this time.

Checking for lumps, I say.

We do our thing. The brown couch is a hide-a-bed. It smells. We sleep there.

In the morning I hate his guts. We eat our Eggos, not talking.

I take the field home.

Mom and Dad are just getting up.

I slept like a log, Mom says, turning the coffee on. I slept like a heroin addict.

I feel great, Dad says. I'll have a light breakfast, and then I'll go rowing. It's such a great day!

I go back to bed. My own bed.

SHATTERED VAGINA

Linda from work. Her departmental emails always go: *Hi everyone!!!!!!!* She has needle track scars. Always long sleeves. I only saw them the once, the staff meeting, when Don said we've all got to roll up our sleeves on this one. And she smiled and did. Really did roll up her sleeves. Nobody talks to her.

I think — I don't know — I think that Linda's from a half-way house or something. And this is her job placement. Last chance or else prison, or forced hysterectomy, I don't know. That sort of thing. I've seen her brown bag lunches. Pepperoni sticks and Coke. Marshmallows. When she asks me to dinner, I can't say no. She might kill herself. Or me.

Her apartment is one grey room with a galley kitchen. Ashtrays everywhere — one on her pillow! — and all of them full up with butts.

We stand in her room. Smiling. She holds out her arms like she's going to hug me. Then pulls back.

Have a seat! she says. Moves an ashtray off the couch. I sit. Purse in my lap.

So! I'm gonna whip up some of my famous pasta with my famous meat sauce! she says. Hope you're not not into meat?

No, I say. I love meat.

Wow. That's so great. So I'm all set to go, and I — shit! Fuck! Fuck me!

I jump in my seat. What's wrong? What is it?

I forgot the parmesan. Fuck meeeee!

It's okay. We don't need it.

No. We do. I'll run and get it.

She runs for the door. Stops.

I'm such a fuckin' lunkhead. I — do you have five dollars I could borrow?

I go in my purse.

I've got oodles of change everywhere. I'll pay you right back in a sec.

Linda goes to the corner store. I get up and look at her bookshelf. Pull one down. A paperback. *Shattered Vagina*. In lipstick letters. I open it.

After he threw me down the stairs, Gord came down to where I was lying in a crumpled heap and cut my bra straps with a paring knife. "Now the little piggie-slut is gonna get her jugs tugged!" he rasped, pulling my bruised breasts. I shivered with fulfillment. I needed all of my holes filled, and filled right then! "I'm gonna

70

*carve ya a new asshole!" Gord said, and in my slut's heart of hearts
I hoped he really would. Sore and torn, I felt like I'd finally 'come
home'.*

I put it back where I found it. I pick up my purse to leave.
Then I think of the work schedule. We're both 8am to 4pm,
all next week. I sit down again.

When she comes back she digs between the couch
cushions for change. I scooch forward so she can root
around me. She finally pours twenty quarters into my
hand.

She pops a cassette into a dusty ghetto blaster. Pointer
Sisters. I sit and listen. She moves pots and pans around in
her little kitchenette.

I did it al dente she says, putting a plate of pasta in front
of me. I wait for her to sit with her plate, then take a bite. It's
crunchy.

So who is Rhonda? Linda says, crunching.

I forget my own name. Then I remember.

Oh. Well. She is who she is. I don't know. I live in the
east end. By the mill.

Oh yeah? Are you married?

Divorced.

Oh yeah? Little ones?

Little ones what? Oh. I —

I could tell Linda my thing with kids. That I had Chlamy-
dia for seventeen years and didn't know it. And I'm sterile. I
could tell her that and she'd understand. Or I could tell her
what I told my mother: my uterus dissolved from when I
had mono.

No. No kids.

Good for you. I have two. They're with my mum. And you know what? I really don't miss them. I really don't. Isn't that awful?

No. At least they're being cared for. Where is your mother?

In hell. With my dead kids. Ha ha. No. Up north. On a farm. It's actually really nice.

I eat what I can.

Thawed out store bought cherry tarts for dessert.

I'm so glad you came over, says Linda. I'm trying to branch out. Reach out in little ways, everyday. Like, even on the bus. I say hi to the bus driver. And then I say thank you when I get off.

The bus service is really good here, I say.

When I go to leave she grabs my arm, gently.

I want to show you something, she says. These things I make.

She goes into the bathroom. Comes out with some sort of necklace. She hands it to me.

I make them myself. A lot of people like them.

It's a string of plastic shells. Ugly as hell.

Thank you! I say. It's gorgeous. It's like a little piece of the Caribbean.

It's twenty-five dollars.

It cost that much to make? I say.

No. You can have it for twenty-five. I'm going to bring 'em to work and sell 'em for forty.

I try to hand it back to her.

Oh. No thank you. It's gorgeous, though.

C'mon, she says. They'll all get snapped up at work.

It's okay. Thanks for dinner.

Please? I'd almost have to say that I'd almost be offended if you didn't buy my art.

I really don't want to buy anything right now. Thank you.

C'mon. It'll spruce up your look.

I don't want your necklace.

I drop it on the couch. I open the door and walk quickly down the hall. What if people from work do buy her shit jewelry? And wear it around the office? What then?

I turn around, fumbling for my wallet. I walk past doors with old plastic Christmas wreaths, doors with worn down welcome mats, trying to remember which one is Linda's.

LISTEN TO THIS

When I come home I take my time putting things away. I assume she's asleep. My wife.

My wife has depression. Nothing has worked, not even shock. She took shock for three months one summer. The only thing that came from that was memory loss. If ever you play 'I remember' with her, she'll keep up unless you remember that summer. Then a blankness will fall over her face and she'll cock her head like a startled dog.

If I'd been thinking, I'd have done more things that summer. Things she wouldn't remember. But I would never do that. I love my wife. She mostly stays in bed. When she gets up I find it jars me. I'm used to the run of the house. Whenever we eat together, I tend to forget to set two sets of cutlery.

I assume she's asleep, but she's not. She calls for me from her bed. I go and sit beside her. I need to change the beds soon.

I'm just spent, I say. I went to Home Depot and it took forever to find the right water filter. And then I did the groceries. Took them to the car in the cart, took the cart back and got my quarter. And as I'm walking back to the car, this *woman*, just a horrible-looking creature, dirty hair all shaved off at the sides, black eye, no teeth of course, barefoot, comes up to me and asks me for change. I'm holding the quarter, so I give her that. Then she calls me girlfriend. Girlfriend! I'm a fifty-year-old man. She says Girlfriend, I didn't sleep a wink last night. It's so hot out. My boyfriend fucked my ass all night long. Now I'm so tired. Rocked me all night — and on and on —

My wife closes her eyes. But I can see that she's listening. She likes to listen.

So I tell the girl I'm sorry she's so tired and keep walking. And she follows me. I'm at the car and she says something like do you like to fuck ass? And I say beg your pardon and she says you can fuck my ass right now, fifty bucks. It's nice and tight for you. I can get fucked and fucked and it still stays tight. So I tell her to please step away from the car. And her eyes just pop — well, at least the one that wasn't swollen shut — and she says, listen to this, she says Whoop de doo! Mister Mini Van! Don't like to fuck ass? Maybe you like to get your ass fucked! Maybe you're an old fag with all his groceries to give to the fag who's gonna fuck your ass! Fuck. Yeah. Bet you've got AIDS, too! Heh? Oh well, that's life. I may have HIV she says, but I sure as shit didn't get it from getting it up the ass like you! Finally I just got in the car. And then she's at the window. Come on down and fuck my ass. Twenty bucks. Nice tight fuck! You totally can't get AIDS when you fuck a lady's ass. We can use a rubber. Come on, girlfriend!

I laugh. My wife turns on her side to face me, eyes closed.

Never seen anything like it. Where did she come from? Poor thing. Anyway, I had a twenty left over from groceries, so I took her in the back and fucked her ass.

She opens her eyes. Deep green, like a cat's.

Just pulling your leg. I drove away and saw her dawdling down the lot to some other poor sod, a woman. Poor thing. Probably sleeps in a bus shelter or something. Anyway. That's my big news for the day. Can you eat something? I went hog wild at Dominion.

No, my wife says. I can't eat a thing.

BURNING LISBON

Mom runs a finger down the catalogue spine. We look at high fashion wigs.

I like the *Affaire Francaise*, she says. But there's also the *Feeling Copper*.

Her legs are crossed. My legs are crossed. Her slipper dangles. Mine are in the wash.

Do I dare buy a wig? she says. I don't need a wig. But I do need a wig. Everyone needs a wig. If someone comes to the door and I'm all ass-backwards.

I look at her hair. Flat and brown. Plastic poodle barrette. We need a wig. And a styrofoam head for it. It will sit on the dresser, like a third little person.

I think the *Burning Lisbon* petite cap would be flattering, I say.

I bet you do, Mom says.

I yawn. I run my hand down my arm. Something like a lump, close to the elbow. Sort of squishy. Sort of sore. Round and smooth like the black enamel earring that Mom lost. That I stole.

I show it to her. The lump.

That's nothing, she says. That's bone. Wandering bone.

In bed. I listen to Mom's ice cubes clink like the bangles on her wrist when she wears 'em. I hear her, talking to herself. Hear her say *Please Jesus and everyone. Don't let my baby have cancer all over his body. Jesus, please.*

Burning Lisbon comes in a bag in the mail. With the *Chatelaine*. And the cable bill second notice.

Burning Lisbon is here! I say to Mom's back.

Who's that? Where? she says to the sink.

The doctor cuts it out. Drops it in a gleaming steel ashtray.

A cyst, he says. I cut one out once, so heavy it had made the guy's head tilt. That's what happens when you're dirty. Are you dirty?

Is he dirty? Mom says, laughing, knees bouncing in her seat. I can't even get him in the tub. Quite often I can smell his backside. People back away from him in Loblaws. Oh, thank you! Thank God!

The wig sits in the bag on the cedar chest. Mom throws it in the laundry basket one day. Now it's in the basement. Some-where.

Mom on the hide-a-bed with the bills. They're going to cut the cable off in ten days, unless. Mom with her drink and the bills. Crying. Shaking her head.

    I can hear her new earrings dingle.

THE BOOKSTORE

The burnt woman stood at the ballet barre in her leotard. She did her bends and stretches, over and over, until the jazzercise class came in.

She undressed herself in full view of the other women in the locker room. Stood nude as she gathered her things. Sat down on a bench to slowly pull on her nylons.

She walked down a busy avenue. Came to a bookstore. People were rushing in and out.

The burnt woman held the door for a small woman, and they both went inside.

The store was dimly lit, for a bookstore. There was a group of people in the cookbook aisle. Men and women. Several wore tams and raincoats. Some were shouting. A woman in a blue vest stood back from the group.

Single file! Shut up! Fuck! Single — shut up! Nancy! said the woman.

The burnt woman got a small coffee from the coffee kiosk. She stood where she could see the small woman. Her little hand, leafing through a big picture book.

The burnt woman scanned the dance and theatre section. She saw a book: *Margot Fonteyn: A Life*. She thought of her books at home, thought she had that book at home. Then she remembered. *The Life of Margot Fonteyn* was the book she had at home. She picked up the new book, gently tucked it under her arm. Kept walking.

Something drew her back to the small woman with the picture book. She stood beside her.

That book looks so lush, said the burnt woman to the small woman.

Mmm hmm, said the small woman.

The burnt woman did a slow pivot on one foot.

I'm Hana, she said.

The little hand kept turning picture pages.

Are you a photographer? asked the burnt woman.

No. Not at all. I'm looking for a gift.

That would make a wonderful gift, said the burnt woman.

The other woman said nothing, kept looking. The burnt woman didn't know what else to say. She was accustomed to standing, in first position, as people stared at her. She was accustomed only to answering questions.

She held onto the shelf, in second position. Sighed a long sigh.

Good gift-giving, she said to the small woman, is, in itself, a gift. Like dance.

I'm not a dyke, said the little woman, not looking up from her book.

The burnt woman put a burnt hand to her chin.

I didn't — neither am I, she said. I was just struck by the lovely book.

A man in a tam and raincoat tore through the aisle.

They fucking ran out of stock! he yelled at them. Some dumb bitch got the last one! Fuck! What's she gonna do with it? I'm a fucking *epicure*! The burnt woman nodded knowingly, and held her own new book close.

WEIGHTS ARE THE DIRTIEST THINGS

Ha. Ugh. Ha. Ugh. Ha. Ugh. Ha. Ugh.

Bench press. Ten pounds beyond my own weight. I weigh a lot. I see the ceiling. Water stains.

The gym is nearly empty. Off to one side of me is a man with his hand on a woman's back. He keeps her straight. She lifts a five pound dumb bell. Smiles at herself in the wall-to-wall mirror.

I leave my towel on the bench. Get a drink from the fountain. Go into the men's. Wash my hands. I wash my hands after every set. Weights are the dirtiest things.

In the mirror I lift my shirt a little. My abs. One of them is bigger than the other ones. The one over my liver. I don't drink. I barely eat.

A stall door opens. I let my shirt drop. Look into the sink.

Look who it is, says the voice behind me.

Mark. From the old gym. He's smiling. Washing his hands. He was fat at the old gym. Wore shirts to his knees that said *Big Boned* and things. He asked me how to use a barbell properly. Always said hi to me.

Now he's thin. Buff. He turns off the tap, tight. A tendon in his forearm. Like the cable in the cable pull.

When did you start here? I say.

The other day. Mickey's burned down.

Mark. Pokey nips. Tight pecs.

Oh. I didn't know that. Arson?

No. Just burned down.

Oh. Well. You look great.

He leans on the soap dispenser.

Thank you. Thank you so much. It's been a real journey. I've shed so many layers. In so many ways.

Cardio, I say. It's so important.

Not even, he says. One day I just thought, Hey! I have a stake in my life! And then the weight just fell off. Also I only eat meat. No carbs. Ever.

We smile and nod. I feel so weak. We smile and nod. Until someone comes into the bathroom.

Later I see him doing preacher curls. At the end he grunts. Shrieks, even. People look.

I think of Mark as I make dinner. Baked salmon. Steamed broccoli. I eat at the coffee table with the TV on. Real Life Miracles. A ninety-year-old woman pulls a truck by a rope in her toothless mouth.

I wasn't going to eat the bread stick. But I do. Eat half of it. With light butter. You need carbs. To live. I love bread.

*

Not so hard, the hairy one says. He wraps his hand around mine. The less hairy one laughs.

You trying to start a fire? he says.

His cock is hot to the touch. Am I? Trying to start a fire?

*

I pile on the plates. I feel strong. A dance song on the intercom. *Don't blow me away! Hey! Hey! Don't blow me away!*

I look around for someone to spot me. It's a lot of weight. A lot more than my own weight.

Mark. Towel wrapped around his neck. I wave him over.

You want me to spot you? Sure thing. Thank you for trusting me!

His wet sweats above my face.

How many reps are we gonna do? he says.

Like, four?

Got it.

Ha. Ugh. Ha. Ugh. My arms shake.

'kay. That's enough.

Nah. You're strong. Gimme two more. Big pecs! Big fuckin' pecs!

I can't hold it up.

Just take it. Help me!

You sure?

His red neck. Other legs coming our way.

Take it!

Two men help him take the weight. One pats me on the back.

Good set, Mark says. I sit up. My towel. From home. Geese on the trim.

I thank him. Look up at him. Tapping on the barbell, to the beat.

I go to the ellipticals for some cardio. The man beside me has the worst B.O. ever. Sweating, cursing at the soccer game on the overhead screen. I do five minutes and have to stop.

The rest of us shower and wear deodorant, I say to him. What makes you special?

I just am. So fuck you, he says.

I shower. My bar soap from home. Unscented. The showers are empty. I soap up and down my crack.

Mark comes in. Buck naked. He never used to shower at Mickey's. Thick, floppy, uncut cock. Big balls.

Howdy, naked stranger! he says.

Howdy, I say.

I try to think of something else to say, over the sound of the showers. But Mark is humming now. Humming and singing, soaping and rinsing.

*

On the phone the guy said do you mind party favours? and I said no, I don't mind party favours. Poppers. A toke or two. He comes through the door, sunburned and all done up in leather. Sits down and starts lining up drug gadgets on my coffee table. Vials of things, a glass pipe.

Just let me get in the zone, he says, picking up the glass pipe. Then we'll be all set. You like piss?

Umm. Sometimes, I say.

He lights his Sailor Moon lighter under the glass pipe. Takes a hit off it.

You want some? You like Tina? he says, passing the glass pipe.

I think of my day tomorrow. The gym. Then work — I've got to do payroll, all kinds of odds and ends. The gym again. Dinner with Julie and Phillip. I take the pipe.

I think of smelling vaguely of piss at the gym, whether sweat will bring out the piss smell.

The guy lights me up. Maybe Mark is into piss, too. Who knows? Who knows what people like?

EVIL

Dick limps from the front to the back of the house. The clothesline. The sheet he shit last night, flapping dry. He felt awful last night. Deathly. Today's he's good to go.

On the lawn, he sees the other side of the sheet. Red sprayed letters. *EVIL*. He looks around. Takes it down.

In the kitchen. *EVIL* spread out on his lap. Who would do that? He's nice to his neighbours. Did he do it himself, in the grip of what made him shit? He goes back over the night, counting off thoughts on his fingers.

He listens. His lot is way back from the road. Bush in the back, on the sides.

A firefly. Then a plane.

He drives. Stops and parks, half in a ditch. Gets out and walks. The red fence. Metal fence. Lilac tree. Stump. Red fence.

She's on her veranda. Her wig.

Ahoy! she says. Waves.

Dick walks along a line of plastic sunflowers to her screen door.

Hi, Judy.

Richard. Look how long your hair is now. When did I see you last?

Last month. In the emerg.

That's right. I'm such a stupid old thing. Always burning myself. Am I a casserole? I wonder!

He grinds a boot heel in the lawn.

I'm so sick of the doctors here, he says. They say I'm rotting. The skin and that.

Oh dear, Judy says. A noble leper. It could be worse. Try to enjoy it. The rotting.

Dick nods.

I just got groceries, he says. Do you want to come for supper?

Judy's eyes close. Coral lids.

You asleep? Dick says, cranes his neck.

Me? I don't sleep. I don't really eat, either. But I'll sit with you. I'll sit with you while you eat your supper. La la!

Dick drives Judy to his house.

Judy turns around in his kitchen.

Dust, she says. I love it. Essential. Dust is like a cozy blanket, spread by angels.

Isn't it?

His head in the fridge. She sits. His ass in her face.

Isn't what?

Dust. Like a blanket. A nice one.

Yeah. Pork chops?

She runs her hand over a glossy knot in the wood table.

I told you. I don't eat.

Okay, he says. I'll eat light, too.

Dick pulls a cabbage from the crisper. Judy sees the *EVIL* sheet.

Did it come that way? The sheet?

He cuts the cabbage in half. Big knife in hand. New. Pearl handle.

No, he says. Someone just did it. The *EVIL*. Kids prob'ly. But who knows? Guess I'm evil, he says. Slit your throat. Heh heh. Put you in the freezer. Then I could really have you for dinner. Heh heh.

Oh! Judy says. You're terrible. Maybe I will have a porked — a chop. A pork chop.

They chew in unison.

There was a weed, Judy says. In my yard. It was so lush. The leaves edged in red. Pretty. I pulled it by the root and ate it.

Uh huh, says Dick.

This was this morning. If it was poisonous, I'd know by now. Don't you think?

Yeah, says Dick.

He drops bones and cold beans into the garbage. Scrapes his plate. Scrapes hers.

The *TV Times* on the counter. Pink post-its stick out, top and bottom. Lots of good shows.

Dick. Looks up from the bones and grounds.

You know, you could be poisoned, he says. We should maybe take you to the emerg.

No, says Judy. No thank you. I'm there enough. The nurses will think I'm lonely and looking. Trying to find dates among the dying. No. Thank you.

What about the Heimlich? says Dick.

What about it? says Judy.

Should I try the Heimlich?

Why? No. No Heimlich.

Why not? says Dick.

Judy shifts in her chair.

For one, the weed is deep in my bowel by now. For two, you might crack my ribs. I'm 82.

Dick wipes down his coffee pot.

I would not. I'd never crack you. You think I think you're a fuckin' egg?

I'm not a bonehead.

Judy holds her hand out.

I know, she says. I know you're not a bonehead. Furthest thing from it.

Alright then, says Dick.

Alright then, says Judy.

NOOK

Mr. J wipes his cock off with paper off a register roll. My knees crack standing up. Gettin' old. 14 in a month.

Get out there, he says. Be hawk-eyed. There's some dirty kids crawling around.

You give me a shout if you see funny business.

The back showroom is dead. I fold a folded hockey sweater. A girl in a bathing suit and miniskirt asks me for the bathroom. It would still smell like jizz so I tell her there isn't one.

Where do you's go when you's have to go? she says.

Her sunburn. Eyes all bloodshot.

We hold it, I say. Go back to my folding.

Mr. J comes out, motions to the front room. We go stand by the cash. Two boys, one with a skateboard under his arm. The tip of his board knocks a box of Whizzers off the shelf.

Sure glad we got those security cameras, Mr. J shouts, looking below the counter at where the monitor would be if we had one. Such a nice, crisp visual, he says.

The boys lope out.

At the foot of the stairs a boy on crutches tugs my shirt. What's up there? he says.

Usually I walk away when someone asks me for help or something. I look at his cast. Nobody's signed it.

There's a bed n' bath nook, a kitchen nook, a baby needs nook, and a more adult novelty nook in the very back.

I sure wish I could go up there, he says.

Yeah. Well. It's not that great. It's boring. It's dumb.

I don't know that. I'd like to see it.

He's little. There's nothing to do but dust.

I guess I could carry you up there, I say.

Okay! I'm way light.

I've never carried anyone. Never even held a baby. My sister has one. She tried to hand it to me once. It started screaming. He's sensitive to smell, she said, taking it back.

I lift him by his pits, to test it out. He is way light. I squat and scoop him up. My knees crack. His crutches crash. I tremble up the vinyl-lined stairs.

At the top of the steps I set him down. He hugs the wall, hops on down the hall. I wait for him.

I could get another summer job. Jerry and Cal work at the marina. They love it. Their hands smell like minnows. They're tanned and tourists sometimes tip them.

My mother wouldn't have it. She says there's prestige to working at the Red Heron Gift Shop. Says it erases some of the bad bits of our family's history. Our welfare days. Our days when Mom gives massages in the basement to mill workers — Mondays, Wednesdays, Fridays and Saturdays.

The kid hops back down the hall.

That was kind of boring, he says. Thanks though.

I pick him up. Halfway down the stairs I feel something. In his pocket. Definitely a naked lady toothbrush. From the adult nook. Always popular.

What was that all about? Mr. J says when the kid hobbles out the door.

He just wanted to see upstairs.

You left the downstairs entirely unattended.

But there's no one else here.

Still. And what's he going to buy?

You never know. I just. I was doing customer service.

Well. Don't. Don't do customer service. You just stand where I tell you.

He's eating Glosette raisins from a box. He pours some into his hand. Want some? he says. I pick one from his damp palm.

We stand at the cash.

MY TREE-TREE

Tree-Tree is sleeping at last. She cried and coughed all morning. I held her, banged her on the back. Tree-Tree. Toe sticking out of the blanket. Poor, black, stinking toe.

I sit on the daybed and open my Bible. *If an animal that you are allowed to eat dies, anyone who touches the carcass will be unclean till evening.*

I don't understand. Does it mean that I've been eating an animal that was still alive? I don't understand. I close my Bible.

I step outside for the mail. Next door has a dog that stares at me when I walk down the driveway. I look in its eyes. See my own death. Hey there, Clipper, I say. Clipper stares, leans a little. Clipper nods. Death.

I care for my loved one and also keep a nice yard. Grass from seed, not sod, and still it's nice, not patchy at all.

The garbage cans by the house, by the hose. I lift the lid on one. A wiener in there. Looks fine. Something inside tells me to eat it. I fish it out. Turn on the hose and give it a rinse off. Eat it.

Make me a hot dog, Tree-Tree says from the bedroom. I gently let the handle on my carpet sweeper fall to the floor.

Hungry? I say. That's good to hear.

Only for a hot dog, she says.

Sure thing. I see you threw some out though.

They were grey and rotten. Go get some new ones.

I pour money from my little silk change purse onto the counter. I count out my loonies and toonies. Back in a jif, I say to my Tree-Tree.

Clipper sits and stays when I walk down my driveway.

At the corner store I buy wieners, buns, mustard. I see some cute stickers by the cash. Little exclamation marks, with smiles in the dot parts. Dancing high heels that sparkle. I smile. I buy them for Tree-Tree. For above her bed.

I walk up my driveway with my bags. Clipper still sitting. He lifts his big black head to the sky. Clipper! I say. He barks. I walk slowly to the door.

Through the picture window I see Tree-Tree. Dancing. Doing spins. Doing the walk-against-the-wind move that the girl did in that concert we saw years and years ago. The girl from Fleetwood Mac.

Tree-Tree stops at the sound of my keys.

You were dancing! I say.

When? she says.

Just now.

I wasn't.

I saw you. It's wonderful!

I wasn't. It was a seizure or something. I can barely walk.

But. You were. Why won't you share this with me?

Share what? Dying and death? Nosey.

I set down my bag on the kitchen table.

Alright. Okay. Do you want your hot dog now? I say.

She grabs the back of a kitchen chair.

Shove it up your fat ass, she says. Do you even know what sickness is like? No. No you do not. It's just a whole other world.

I know, I say. I know what an awful journey this is.

I wish I was sicker. You wouldn't even know me. There'd be no chit-chat.

She hugs the walls back into the bedroom.

I put things away. I tuck the stickers away for another day.

I hear her in bed, crying. Coughing. I go in my own room and shut the door.

I lie still on my little bed. I pray.

Dear Heavenly Father.

Thank you for such abundance in my life.

Thank you for Tree-Tree's healing.

I ask that you let Tree-Tree share her healing with me.

I ask that when you answer my prayers, that I know about it, I say to myself, but don't pray it.

It's raining now. Clipper hates the rain. He'll howl 'til it stops. He'll howl like hell, but nobody will bring him in.

UNCOMMON PINK SOFTNESS

I drive home. Almost miss my own driveway.

    We've been getting hang-up calls, Toddy says. We got hang-up calls at 1:17,

    2:05, 2:30 and 3.

    Was there a voice?

    No voice. Just a bit of breathing. And hang-ups.

    Did it sound like a man breathing or a woman?

    A man. Or a woman.

    Must've been your father. Or your aunt.

    Guess what time it is now? he says. He's on the table. Guess the time and don't look. Guess. Just guess it.

    I have no idea. Five o'clock.

    No. I can bend all my fingers right back.

I put him in front of TV. I sit down and do the grocery list. Takes forever. Toddy's allergies. Last week I gave him a Pop-Tart and his lips and eyelids went all ballooney. In the car today I went into my purse, tried to touch up my lip liner with his EpiPen. Took a bit before I realized.

And there's my diet. 60 pounds in three months. I have to be tough with myself. Little bites. Or nothing. I swoon lifting the laundry basket. I kind of like it. I have to be tough.

Phone rings. I answer. Breathing. Hang-up. I do *69. A number I don't know. I call it.

Duffy's, says a woman.

What's Duffy's? I say. You've been calling here.

Duffy's is Duffy's. Dry cleaning.

Well. Please stop calling.

Don't worry. Fuck you.

Fuck you! Who is this?

My name is Kay. Do you want to talk to my supervisor?

No, I say. I don't want to talk to anyone. Ever. Just please don't call here.

Don't worry.

That was funny, Toddy says. I hold him by the arm and lock the front door.

In Dominion I get a basket, then trade it for a cart. I push past big boxes of watermelon. Toddy follows me.

Where the toilet paper is, a man and woman hold hands, compare the two-ply kinds.

This one is soft, says the woman. Like, uncommon soft. It's so worth it.

And it's pink, says the man. Your ass needs uncommon pink softness.

I get the kind I get. The one with the black woman holding the black baby on the plastic.

Toddy wants smoked salmon fillets. His throat would close in a heartbeat. I smack his hand away.

Can corn. Can peaches. The cart's got a bum wheel. I jerk it back, push ahead.

I pass the magazine rack. That girl, on the front of the gossip rag. That girl from that show where she kept getting fired, but in a funny way. She's on the front with her husband. Her husband who fell off a boat and got brain damage. *Sex has never been better!* it says beside the picture of her hugging him. His tongue hanging out.

I look at the picture. Look and look. My hair's half grey. I've never been to a dentist.

The plants and flowers nook, by frozen goods. Carnations galore. Little, droopy yellow flowers in plastic canoes. I feel dizzy.

The girl on the intercom. She says Toddy's name. I look around. A man in a blue vest walks my way. Hand in hand with Toddy.

Thank God, I say to him. I've been frantic. Where was he?

Ah. Just snooping about down at the other end. No problemo.

His brown eyes and nice, feathered hair.

Thank you so much, I say. Can I pay you?

No. God no. We get buckets of lost kids. Should have a lost kid aisle.

I put my hand on his hand on Toddy's hand. The man takes his hand away. Says, There ya be. Gives me a soldier salute. Walks away.

Where did you go to? I say.

I've been around, Toddy says.

I have to pee. Mummy has to pee, I say.

Toddy in the women's with me. He watches me pee. It's good to sit. Less dizzy.

Get some toilet paper for Mummy, I say.

Why? he says. To eat it?

Ha ha. I need to wipe the pee off. Speaking of eating though. What'll we have for supper?

I wipe up and think of our groceries outside the door. The cart full up and I can't think of a thing to feed him. Or me. Especially me.

THREE BEARDS

Snow. We're in our old car, that was new when we bought it. We're both full up from supper. We ate at Mama Hunka's Place. Shoveled it in, not talking, with plastic forks and knives. Last bite, Bill broke a prong on his fork. I looked up. Kept eating.

We're still not talking, here in the car. On the radio is a woman who was kept in a crate for three years by her husband, then escaped and wrote a play about it.

I couldn't move, in my crate, she says, but my imagination was free. Like a dove.

I'd like to read the stage directions for that play, Bill says.

I lean away from him. The rubber hula girl on the dashboard. She sticks in the cold and can't hula, can only lurch a little. We got it at a yard sale. Guy tried to stick

109

the quarter change down my shorts. And I let him. Bill didn't mind. The guy was in a wheelchair. And Bill wouldn't mind anyway.

A whirring sound. Our old car. Rust on the hood. Dead 8-track. When he drives me to work, I make him stop the block before. I jump out, look around. Try to look like I just escaped from being kidnapped.

Bill's swearing. Saying things about the engine. I don't listen. Then he says, watch that gauge there. It should be in the middle. But it's closer to the H, H is for hot. Keep watching it. I've gotta shit so bad. Keep watching it.

I keep watching it. I watch it like a motherfucker. The pointer goes past the H. I watch the pointer go past the H.

Bang under the hood. The sound is like the time all our fisting pornos fell off the bookshelf. We look at each other. We both wear glasses too big for our face.

We wave and wave. Smile and wave. Nobody stops for us. I sit in the car. Get out of the car. Lean on the car like a mechanic's pin-up. Walk along the roadside. Broken beer bottles in the snow. I could go for a beer.

I come back to the car and stare at Bill's fat ass as he leans over the engine. If the hood was a big blade and it fell, he'd be cut clean in half. I think of his halves. Laid out on the road's shoulder. 'Coons and crows eating away.

A black car with three bearded men in it slows down beside us. The driver winks at me. Nice car. New car. Not rusty.

A pain, in my head. A lot of people in my family had strokes. Even kids — one of them mid-wish over her own birthday cake.

I get in the car with the beards.

Driving down the main drag.

Aren't you something? one of them says.

You like group? says the driver.

Group what? I say. But I know what he means.

Group fun. We're looking for group.

Sure. I like group. I love group.

You been in lots of groups? says the third beard.

Here and there.

Hot. Here, do this.

The beard beside me hands me the little bottle. I take a whiff. My head pounds. I look around. Everything is sexy. Sexy dash. Sexy ashtray. Sexy seatbelt.

The beard undoes my parka. My shirt. My flabby tits. Bypass scar.

Real man! he says. Real life! Real lived-in! Right on!

He rolls up a sleeve. A rash. Brown and red scales. I take a hit off the little bottle. Sexy rash.

At a red light I look over at the next car. Bill, with a black man. Bill rocking in his seat, to the music in the car. I'm sure there's no music in the car.

When I was a bartender I'd get dozens of phone numbers. Business cards, scraps of napkin. I'd forget them in my pockets, doing laundry. They'd come out of the dryer in one hard lint lump.

I think of all the dirty dishes at home. It's his turn to do them and he'll do them. If I have to pile them all on his side of the bed. If I have to shake my fat fist in his fat face.

LUUUUUUVE

There's space left over at the end of *Superman 2*. It taped a bit of a news show, about a mother who wanted to marry her son, then killed him when he said no. She's speaking from prison. She has a carnation corsage pinned to the top of her prison jumpsuit.

It's like when friends start to get with each other, she says. Smiling, shrugging her skinny shoulders. You start out as one thing and then comes the lightbulb and BAM! you just get with them. It's something called *Luuuuuuve*.

Trina rolls over in her patch of sunlight on the floor. She's cracking her toe knuckles, bending back each stubby toe 'til it pops. That is so pukey, she says. With that fat, lolling tongue of hers. If they had a baby, it would prob'ly be one big oval with no arms or legs, she says.

Pukey is not a word, Mum says, tying off the ends on a doll dress she's just finished. She makes doll dresses, then puts them in the towel cupboard.

The tape has been taped over so many times that the prison mum's littlest son sounds like a man with gigantism when he looks into the camera and says, When are you coming back from the store, Mommy?

The medicine chest is open a bit when I go in to wash my hands for supper. I look in there and there's a little metal cup on the shelf. I've never seen it before. It's not from the kitchen, it's not one of Trina's crappy things. I bring it up to my face. It smells like the basement. At the bottom of the cup is a decal, partly peeled off, of a happy baby's face, licking its lips like it's waiting for a cupcake or a cookie, something good to eat.

Also, in the mirror, something else I've never noticed before. Half my face is red for no reason. Red like I've been smacked.

When's Trina going to move out? That's what I think to myself, Mum and Dad too, probably, whenever we all sit down to eat. Almost 20, and all she does when she comes home from her daycare job is walk around the house in her track pants, picking at herself. Her upper arms are all scabbed over. Once, late at night, I heard Mum telling Dad that she sometimes worries that Trina's going to end up dead.

Trina takes the biggest piece of fish for herself and pours ketchup on it. Mum lights a cigarette. She hardly ever eats with us. She eats later, in the dark, standing over the sink. Dad turns on the radio. The end of a woman singing really fast, in French.

Hey Dad, Trina says with her mouth full, if you were going to molest one of us, which one would you fuck?

What is wrong with you? How can you come up with shit like that? And don't ever say fuck in this house. You. You just get out of my sight!

Dad's temples roll and gnaw.

I'm not saying I want you to do me! I was just asking. It was just something to say.

Well, it's a terrible something to say, Mum says. We're not sitting in hell, are we? This is supper. She turns up the radio. Long range forecast.

I guess I'm not allowed to talk, Trina says. Rolls her eyes.

I look down at her lap. Thighs all flat and spread out on the chair. I kind of hope Dad will hit her.

He grabs her plate instead. From his seat he throws it in the sink. Peas go flying. Mum picks one out of her hair, turns away and eats it. I take my first bite of fish.

After sports and traffic, Dad flicks off the radio and we sit in silence, forks against porcelain, finishing up.

Did you know that in Nazi times they made the Jewish families do that to each other? Mum says finally, getting up to plug in the kettle for tea. They made the Jewish mother have sex with the Jewish son, and the Jewish father with the Jewish daughter, at gunpoint. That's a fact. How would you like that?

Now, if you smarten up a little, we'll have some tea.

I know everyone has wished this at one point or another, but when I look at her — the wide face, small teeth, the crow's feet she's already getting — and, of course, the way she thrills over stuff that's already old news to the rest of us, I really do believe it about Trina: adopted, switched at birth, or at the very least, not my Dad's. Whenever she's home the house feels like a motel. Open, in a bad way. She just misses the mark, and she thinks that makes her more interesting. Or more *something*. We know better. That time I heard Mum in bed, whispering to Dad about Trina ending up dead — did she really say I worry or I wish?

SHALIMAR

Look at it, she says, lifting her top. Look at what a mess it is, she says, cupping what's left. Can you stand it? It's like a horror movie. What can I do about it?

I don't know, I say. She still looks good. Last time I saw her naked was at a bridesmaid dress fitting. I held the dress to my chest so nothing showed. She trotted out naked. Not even panties. The sales girl came. Saw Nan naked. Stared. There was something about her body even then. I go to the sink. Move a plate.

It's good, I say. It's almost artful. At least they got it all. What perfume are you wearing?

Shalimar. It covers the puke stink.

I adore it. It makes me feel like I'm on a gondola, drunk. Or something.

What's a gondola again? Oh yeah. Huh. I feel sick. I'm always hot.

I sit at the kitchen table.

Her husband comes home. Slips off his shoes all delicate, like an old lady. Hi Anna, he says to me. Hairy hand on my shoulder.

Well, if yours is home, mine is home, I say. I pick my purse. Kiss Nan on the forehead. Her hot, white skin.

On my way home I buy Shalimar. In the car I spray and spray. It gets in my eyes. I cry Shalimar for a minute. Then drive home.

He's in my catering apron. My only good one. Nan called, he says. Running a bowl of something under the tap.

Did I leave my purse? I say as I look at my purse.

She said she took a turn. She said she threw up and it was like meat that came out. She wants to know if you'll make supper for them.

Why can't he do it?

I'll do it, he says. I've already started.

I look over his shoulder at what's in the bowl.

Gypsy stew, he says. Lots of good things all thrown together. Very fortifying.

Do you even know what you're doing? Have you made it before? Ever?

I'm trying something new.

You're so inventive. Just don't burn the fucking house down.

I slip past him.

What are you wearing? he says. It's nice.
It's Nan's. I say.

I'm in the mirror of my walk-in closet. Take my top off. Pull my breasts apart. Try to tuck one under my arm. Smile at myself. If something of mine — a tit, a finger — got cut off, would I feel loss? Or would I feel lighter?

I think of them cutting away at Nan. Limb by limb, 'til she's only a head. I could cradle her, the head. Take her everywhere I ever go.

OH!

My partition, and the things I've tacked to it. The Kim Carnes ticket stub. The little picture of John Stamos with no shirt. The card from everyone here, the year I turned 30. I'm 36 now.

My boss walks past. She had a baby last year, but hasn't lost the weight. She used to walk fast and scan the room as she went. Now she walks slower, and always looks down and sort of to the side.

I get up quick. My chair goes rolling back on its rollers. It bumps Sandra, in her chair. She goes Oh! then goes back to her calculator. Pounds the keys, pound, pound, pound. Her haircut is long on one side, short on the other. Her rusty pedal bike locked up out front.

I go to the bathroom. Lock myself in a stall. I'm not happy today, like I could be. And have been. Like I am usually.

I stand in the stall. I smell crap. Turn around. Beside the bowl is a coil of crap.

I look away. It's not even noon. I smell the crap and press my face to the stall door.

Dale sat on my loveseat. He was small and pale. His picture online made him look tanned and Italian.

One eye wandered. We spoke and one eye stared at my end table.

Can I get you a drink? I said.

Do you have any milk? he said.

I thought he meant breast milk. When we chatted online, I asked him what kind of women he found attractive.

I like my women docile, he wrote. *But not door-matty. I like them to be like Weebles. Remember Weebles? Weebles will wobble but they won't fall down? I like my women to wobble a little. And, of course, pregnant women are always very radiant and compelling.*

So. I thought he meant breast milk. Which I don't have, of course. But he meant milk. Which I didn't have.

Sorry. No milk, I said.

Orange juice, then? he said.

I went to my fridge. I took the pitcher of juice in both hands. Poured juice into my brass goblet. Saw my face in the slick yellow pool.

Just put it on the coffee table, he said when I brought him his juice.

I did as he said. He tugged at his belt buckle. I looked up at the ceiling. The swirls and stars I painted there. From a kit I bought.

What are we gonna do about this? he said.

I looked down from the stars. His thing in his hand. The kind that still has the skin.

I dropped to my knees. Ran my hand down his thing. Felt for his balls. There were none.

Oh, I said.

I had cancer, he said. Is that a problem?

I wanted to run. Out my own door, down the hall, down the stairs, through the lobby and onto the street.

No, I said. Of course not.

Get to work, he said.

I took his thing in my mouth. With my right hand I grabbed at his missing balls. Cupped them, petted. Tickled them. His phantom balls.

This went on for awhile.

Oh my god Sandra, I say, have you seen the bathroom?

She goes all stiff in her seat.

Where? she says.

Here, I say.

No.

I make gasp and chuckle sounds. Shake my head. It's something to talk about, with Sandra.

She puts her hands up in front of her. Like she's checking her nails.

Fuck you, she says. Why would I shit on the floor?

My jaw drops. I make a motion with my hand. Like I'm petting her hair.

I totally didn't say that, I said. I just wondered if you saw it. I'd never think —

Everyone is just so fucking vengeful, she says, cutting me off. Do you know what? It's like, you can't even do one thing without everyone wanting to kill you, she says.

She looks at me. Her shirt has horses on it. Two thin brown streaks on a breast, in between horse heads. Reigns, I guess. Or coffee stains.

Nobody wants to kill you, I say. I just wondered if you saw it. The shit.

Sandra tilts her head. Shuts her eyes. Starts to cry.

I sit in my chair, wheel a little her way.

Oh, she says. Leans her head on me. The side of her head with short hair.

Oh. Fuck. Cindy, she says. Cindy. You fucker, Cindy.

There are no Cindys in the office. I put my hand on her damp back.

Sandra, I say, could I get you a glass of water?

Shit. Sorry, she says, pulls back. Yeah. Could I have some water?

In the kitchen, by the water cooler, my boss is massaging her breasts. Not looking at me.

What's up with Sandra? she says.

I get a glass. Nudge past her and her boobs. I hear her rough skin run down velour. The glass fills. I look up at my boss.

I think Sandra is ill, I say. I think she may have had a bowel movement on the floor.

In the office? she says.

No, in the bathroom. And now she seems kind of confused.

My boss sighs.

Should we call an ambulance? she says.

I don't think so, I say. Maybe just send her home.

Christ. This day has been endless. Okay. You walk her home, then. She's just down the street, isn't she?

Is she? I say.

I think so, she says. Sandra? Yeah. She's down the street and a bit east.

Sandra drinks her water, then gets her bag and bike helmet from her locker.

I walk with her. We don't talk. Outside it's scorching. Car hoods cast blinding light. I'll walk with her, and then it'll be one o'clock. When four comes, I'm going to cab it home, strip off, turn on my little window air conditioners, the good and the bad one, and just lay on my loveseat all night. Maybe see who's online. See if anyone's sent me fun email.

MRS. PARK

In my room, curtains shut, I play my one and only 45. *Won't you take me to Funkytown?* I sing and dance. My friend gave me the 45. My only friend. Gone for the summer. Her mom made her go to a fat farm, when she broke a lawn chair. Canada Day, plastic flag in hand.

Are you talking to me? Mrs. Park says.

No. I'm singing.

Oh. Are you singing to me? Are you my beau?

No.

Lunch is ready.

Salmon sandwiches, cut in half. Well, nearly in half. Two-thirds and one-third. Mrs. Park is part blind. Once she made me Kraft Dinner with chocolate milk.

I sit at the table where Dad sits. Mrs. Park sits where Mom sits. She chews a lot before she swallows. So she doesn't choke. She says she's nearly choked to death a dozen times. Twice on wedding cake, her first and second marriage. I don't dare marry again, she says. Third time lucky or third time dead? Who can say? she says.

I guess you'd like to play Frisbee, she says. I'm sorry I'm not a young girl.

I hate Frisbee. I hate games.

Good! Me, too! I'll eat to that.

There's one dill pickle left.

Do you want that pickle? Mrs. Park says.

No.

I should let you have it. I'm just a greedy old woman.

You can have it.

Thank you. Please don't tell your mother. I need this income so badly.

I put the dishes in the dishwasher. Mrs. Park pours a glass of Pepsi. Stirs in something from one of my Dad's bottles from the back of the cupboard. Goes into the den and turns on the TV.

I lie on a pillow on the floor. We watch Coronation Street. She gets up and goes back in the kitchen. I hear ice cubes and fizz.

What did I miss? she says.

I don't know. The ugly lady behind the bar started crying. Then it was a commercial.

She was crying? Why was she crying? They say it's good to cry but I don't think so. I've been crying all my life. My boy passed away. You know how?

No.

He was on drugs. They call it Angel Dust but I say it's Devil Dust. Yuh.

He dived into a pool with no water in it. This was '73. Then my husband run away with a Black, that winter. I've been crying ever since. Yuh. You promise me you won't get all mixed up with drugs and druggies. You promise me that.

I move up a little on my pillow.

Okay. I promise.

My back is to her, but I can hear her get up again. Then two old nyloned feet, one on each side of me. Heavy breath parts my hair. She's standing over me with her drink.

You go get that record you were playing, she says.

What record?

The one you was playing, before lunch.

What record?

I'll cry. Don't make me cry. You go on and get that record and we'll dance.

I go get the record. Put it in its paper picture sleeve. Carry it carefully into the den. Take it out of its paper picture sleeve. Put it on the big stereo.

Whoah! A-dingle doo! A-dingle-doo! says Mrs. Park, dancing to my music.

She points her toes. Makes toe-dents in the plush rug.

Take my hands, she says. Spin me 'round, lover!

I don't want to take her hands. It's daylight out. I don't like her. I only dance alone. Except for with my fat friend. Who's gone. I take her hands. Try to spin her around. She's taller than me. Has to squat a bit to turn under my arm. Spills her drink a little. Pepsi splotch on the plush beige.

And then the funkytown! A-dingle doo! Here we go!

I pull away from her. She keeps spinning. Then she stops spinning. Stands there, swaying.

Oh dear. I feel a little off. Not good. Not good at all.

Maybe sit down, I say.

Ho. I feel like it's going to come out both ends.

Mrs. Park runs to the bathroom. I grab the remote and flip through the channels — nothing on. I turn it off.

Mom comes home. Her keys clink against the kitchen table.

Hello? Everyone still alive? Hello?

Hi, I say.

Mum comes into the den. Her new perm. Tinted a rust colour. Rust like the slipcovers on every chair in the house.

Where's Mrs. Park? she says.

I'm in here, Mrs. Davis, calls Mrs. Park from the bathroom, door open.

Oh. Okay! Mom says to her. How long has she been in there, she says to me.

I want to say all day. She's been in there all day, since you left. But I don't get the chance.

Mrs. Davis, come in here! says Mrs. Park. It's black! It's black like a coal that's been in the fire! For a hundred years! Come and look! Oh God!

Mom looks at me. I look at Mom. We walk slowly to the bathroom. The sound is crying and the needle skipping on the run-out of my one and only record.

LOVE IS THE WRONG KIND OF NUANCE

A cigarette butt, stuck in the earth of my window box garden. Between my neat pink pansies, it looks like the dead bulb of something. How did it get there? I'm fourteenth floor. I don't smoke. I don't have friends who smoke. I don't have friends, period.

I feel my balls. Roll 'em, squeeze 'em. Make 'em bounce. My lover had ball cancer. Went thru chemo and turned into a poet. I'm governed by nuance now, he'd say all the time. He moved out when I was away at my mum's. Left a note: *Love is the wrong kind of nuance for me right now*, it said. He took my camcorder.

I'm feeling my balls for lumps.

I felt my balls at work. My job was cashier at a place that sells special, all-weather sweaters. People, men and women, came in and tried them on. It was a novelty thing that never stopped being novel. Someone would drag a friend in, saying try it, just try it on. When they did, they'd say things like I don't feel hot, but I don't feel cold, or, I could wear this all year 'round. And you could.

I got fired. Not for feeling my balls. For crying. A little girl came into the store with her mother. Little girl's shirt went down to her ankles. On the front it said *You don't know me well enough to hate me*. So much anger in the world. I ran crying to the bathroom. There was a line-up at the cash.

My boss was a tiny woman with crab hands. When she was thinking about something, she made her thumb and pointer pinch together, over and over. Crabby crab crab. She wasn't doing the pinching thing when she said, end of the day, is everything all right at home? I hope so. I worry about you, and not just today. You're a good person. I hate to see you in pain. I think, in many ways, we're kindred spirits. I have a lamp at home that simulates sunshine. I've never felt better. They have them at 4You, other end of the mall. Unfortunately, we've come to the end of our working relationship at this time.

I asked her why.

Please don't advance on me. I'm a small woman and you're a big man. I feel your threat.

I'm not advancing on you, I said.

Please don't make me call mall security. Thank you and goodbye.

I want to go home. To where I was born. I was a home birth. My mother had a mid-wife come in to keep the hair out of her eyes and tell her to push. Supposedly all she did was sit in the corner and smoke. Mum said she did it all herself. At home. With the radio on full blast.

Called her last night. It rang and rang. She's always home. I thought she was dead on the floor. When she answered, her mouth was full of food.

Were you eating? I said.

Not really. My guts are in knots.

How come.

There's a paranoid schizophrenic just moved in with his folks next door. Straight from the nuthouse. I just get comfortable and he starts screaming. I hope he doesn't hack me up for the hell of it.

I'm sure he's medicated, I said.

Yeah, well, I'm not. Thought I'd try to eat something. Might as well stuff myself with newspaper.

Huh. So. I thought I might come home for awhile.

Good. Yeah. At least it'll be two against the wacko. Plus there's a pow-wow at school next weekend. I just love that fried bread they make. Maybe that'll stay down.

Another lover, years ago, he thought he felt a lump. Doctor said what he felt was not a lump, was only an inflamed follicle. We went camping.

Our first night in the tent, he made me feel his bad ball. It was twice the size of the other one.

That's not normal, he said.

It's not? I said. I thought one ball was supposed to be bigger. Like right hand, left hand.

But one nut is nut-sized and the other's like an apple.

I like it, I said, doing my thing on him. He screamed when I took the apple nut in my mouth.

I go home to my mother. I take the bus. The driver tour-guides us all the way. On your left is Red Lake. Here we have the Mather Walls House. As if we all don't know. As if we all don't take this hour-long route all the time.

Mum makes me bacon and eggs and toast from old bread. Watches me eat. Closely. Her eyes follow my hand to my mouth to my plate again.

Tired from your trip? she says.

So tired.

There's lots of your father's old pajamas in the basement if you want. Watch out for the one with the shit stains, though.

I don't wear pajamas.

Alright then. So, I'm going out.

But I just got here.

And you're tired. And I'm not. I'm going out.

Where?

I don't know. We'll see.

She looks a bit crazed. She was wearing a baseball cap and slapping her hand against the wheel when she picked me up at the bus depot. She threw open the passenger door so hard that it shut again.

I go to bed.

I wake up when she comes home. I can faintly hear giggling.

Tomorrow I'm going to go to the beach. Sit on a blanket. Tan 'til I burn.

I can do something wrong here. Cruel, illegal even. And it would still be alright. A man my mother knows barely got off for feeling little Indian boys' asses, but people still go to his restaurant.

At the beach I'll think of things to do.

I call her into my room. She sways in the doorway. Plops down on the edge of the bed.

I don't feel well, I say.

Where? she says. Sitting. Swaying.

I don't know.

Come downstairs, she says.

But I don't feel well. I need — I don't know.

She stands up and puts out her hand. Come downstairs and join us, she says.

Us?

I don't want to know. I try to fall asleep again. Bunch a bed sheet between my thighs. It's cool in the house, but I'm sweating. I've always been a sweater. I never could model the all-weather sweaters like the other workers at the sweater place. People would think that the all-weather sweaters weren't all-weather after all, because I'd be all wet with sweat.

Mum with two women her age. They're all barefoot. Drinking rum and cokes. One of them is wrapping a long string around tin cans.

And if he trips over my booby trap and says he hears voices, Mum says to her friends, I'll say 'You sure do! My voice! My voice saying fuck right off, wacko!' And I'm gonna get a handgun, too!

They all laugh. They all look up.

Is that him? Is that the wacko? says the tin can one.

No, no. That's my boy!

My mother throws up her arms.

Welcome to the war zone, kiddo! she says. Suit up and fall in!

GRAB AND GRAB

Two kimonos. The blue dragon one and the lily pad one with the lightning piping. Slippers, of course. Drawstring everything. Belts dig into me, make me tense. A vacation should be soothing. It has to be, this coming one.

The way that little nothing-special pressed my hand to his hot face. Then told me he was working. Working! That's not work. That's a kind of assault.

Toiletries I'll leave out 'til the last minute. One cologne. An aftershave. Liquid soap packets wrapped in beach things. A spill and my swimsuit's a goner. As they say.

I write out a note for Leona. Where the cat food is, when to feed the cat. Flannery likes lipstick, will eat a whole tube then puke and poo auburn. I put that in the note — don't leave lipstick out.

My note paper says *a note from me*. After *from me* I put *Flannery*. Write it all from her point of view. Feed me. Brush me. I like lipstick — careful!

I look out past the lip of my tub. Ants. From out of the furnace vent. Ants. Ants galore. Not red ants. White ants. Pink ants. I think: is the white the baby of the pink? Or what?

I step out of the tub. Wad up toilet paper. Squat.

I dab at the ants. They don't die. Just run faster. Like they like it.

I pull on the roll again. Grab the towel. The facecloth. The sweater on the hook in the hall. The tea towel from the kitchen. I can't travel with ants in the house. Grab and grab and grab.

I get angry. I pull back to punch the mirror. I see how anger brings out the fat in my face. My nose — I've had it thinned. My hairline restored. It all looks terrible. My whole face is a lawsuit.

And then there's the slant of my floor here, here and all over! I feel like I'm already on the cruise ship, it's so slanted. Don't get me started. On the slant. Do not get me started.

A trip by sea. I must be crazy. Lacking something upstairs. I hate the water.

Sherry in a soup cup. A half a thing of red wine in the back of the fridge. I look and think young for my age. I keep an open heart. My last courtship. Fun. His septic shock. Sad. The hair on his toes.

Lysol in the cupboard. The cologne I've left out of the bag. I could drink those things. I go and hold the Lysol. Hold it like a diamond goblet. Smile. Never would I do that.

My tickets. Passport. Pamphlets. Spread out on the chopping block, in a fan. Always an eye for the decorative. I'm a surprise to myself.

Thank you's: Zoe Whittall, Ann Decter, Hal Niedzviecki, Shary Boyle, Ken Sparling, Derek McCormack, Jean McKay, David Hawe, Ruby Rowan, Julie DiCresce, Kim Erskine, Sharon Achtman, Caroline Azar, Adrienne DeFrancesco, Paul Gallant and everyone at PTP, Dick Kearney, Jan McMillin, and a bell-like shout out to Rob Matte.

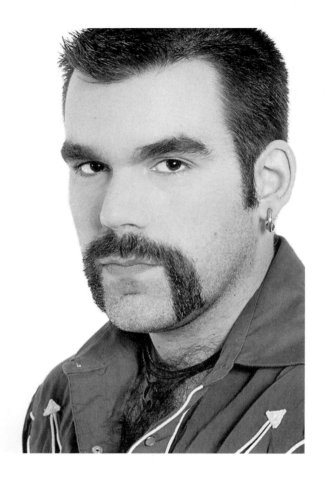

GreG Kearney was born and raised in Kenora, Ontario. His first play was produced when he was 17. His last play was produced in 2002 and received terrible reviews. He's resident humor columnist at *Xtra!* magazine and his fiction has appeared in several leading lit journals. He lives in Toronto. *Mommy Daddy Baby* is his first book.